Tuchali*

By Cindy K. Stone
Illustrated by Natasha Evans &
Kevin O'Connell

To Katelyn, Jacey & Julia

* **tuchali**, n., a piece

A dictionary of the Choctaw language; by Byington, Cyrus, 1793-1868; Smithsonian Institution. Bureau of American Ethnology; Swanton, John Reed, 1873-1958; Halbert, Henry S. (Henry Sale), 1837-1916

Share a tuchali of your heart daily.

Nobody saw it happen,
but this is 100% true.

On the day you were born
a piece of my heart
went
with
you.

And since then
'til forever…

Wherever you go and
whatever you do
that little piece of my heart
will be there with you, too.

You can…

Go to the moon
in a big balloon,

Swim like a seal
on a wavy
afternoon,

Climb a mountain in the Shenandoah,

Dance
on stage
with a
feather boa,

12

Run a cross country race
'til your face is red,

Or recuperate in
a hospital bed,

And still...

17

Wherever you go and
whatever you do
know that little Tuchali of my heart
is there with you, too.

A heart can be a magical thing,
like a circle, never ending.

With each piece shared
it somehow grows bigger,
like a flower blooms from a seed.

And no matter what
that Tuchali follows you
your whole life through,

Shelter you on a rainy day,

and keep you warm
when the sun's away;

Strengthen your courage
when fear creeps in,

help you choose wisely,
stay focused, and win!

Let you love freely,
like a bird in the sky,

28

connected
to all heaven
and earth,
even as
you fly.

Always know,
wherever you go and
whatever you do,
there is peace in my heart
knowing that tiny Tuchali
is with you.

This is 100% true.
As true as the day you
were born.

31